Heverly

Heverly

KEVIN YAGHER

SEASTAR BOOKS
NEW YORK

"Shhh . . ." whispered Eli. "Did you hear that?" Eli and Isabel crouched together in a tangled thicket, peering out at the woods around them. Eli strained to listen for the sound of padded footfalls on dry leaves. There were many things that might be hunting them in this forest outside the kingdom of Heverly—badgers, ferrets, even the wild forest cats, quick and fierce as lightning.

"I don't hear anything," Isabel whispered.

"Maybe it was nothing." Eli smiled, a bit chagrined. "These days, I jump at every sound. I think it's safe now." Isabel followed him out of the thicket, shaking her clothes free of the thorns, but then she paused with a hand on his arm.

"Eli . . . run!" she shouted as a low growl reached their ears.

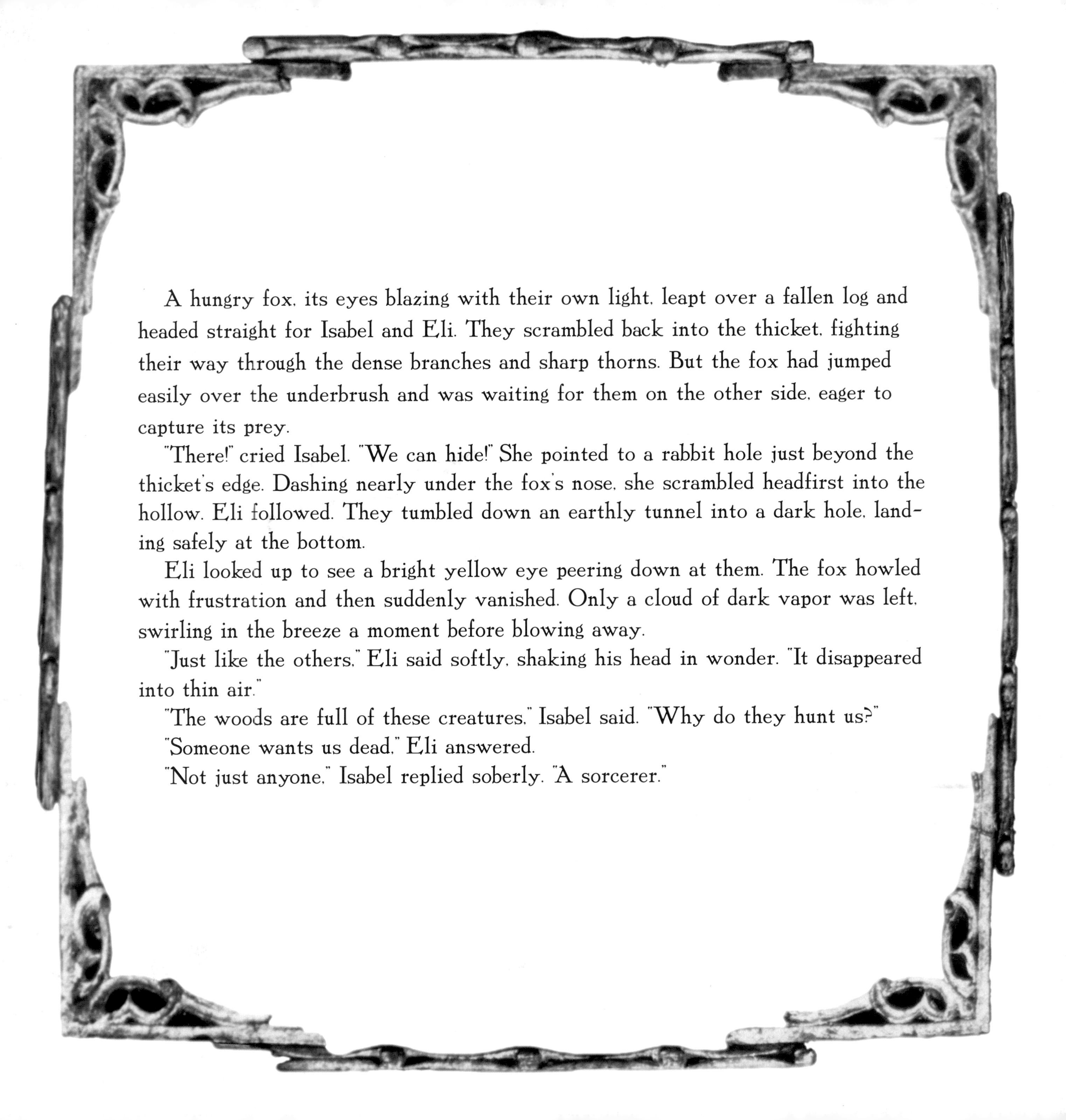

A hungry fox, its eyes blazing with their own light, leapt over a fallen log and headed straight for Isabel and Eli. They scrambled back into the thicket, fighting their way through the dense branches and sharp thorns. But the fox had jumped easily over the underbrush and was waiting for them on the other side, eager to capture its prey.

"There!" cried Isabel. "We can hide!" She pointed to a rabbit hole just beyond the thicket's edge. Dashing nearly under the fox's nose, she scrambled headfirst into the hollow. Eli followed. They tumbled down an earthly tunnel into a dark hole, landing safely at the bottom.

Eli looked up to see a bright yellow eye peering down at them. The fox howled with frustration and then suddenly vanished. Only a cloud of dark vapor was left, swirling in the breeze a moment before blowing away.

"Just like the others," Eli said softly, shaking his head in wonder. "It disappeared into thin air."

"The woods are full of these creatures," Isabel said. "Why do they hunt us?"

"Someone wants us dead," Eli answered.

"Not just anyone," Isabel replied soberly. "A sorcerer."

Eli and Isabel climbed cautiously out of the rabbit hole. Seeing no sign of the fox or any other threat, they began to make their way back to the abandoned bird's nest that had been their home since they had left Heverly.

As they walked through a breezy meadow, Isabel took Eli's hand.

"It's been nearly two seasons since we left the kingdom," she said to Eli. "Don't you think your father has forgiven us by now? If we return, surely he would allow us to marry."

Eli shook his head. "My father would rather give up his throne than allow the crown prince to marry—"

"A servant's daughter," Isabel finished for him. "Your father is a proud man, Eli, but he loves you. Perhaps, after all this time . . . "

They passed under a spray of hanging jasmine, and Eli lifted his head to breathe in its sweet fragrance. "My mother loved that scent," he said sadly. "If she were still alive, she would have softened my father's heart."

Before Isabel could reply, a shadow fell across them.

Looking up, they saw a giant dragonfly with translucent wings hovering high above them. "Run, Isabel!" Eli cried. He snatched up some rocks lying at his feet. But to his surprise the dragonfly spoke.

"I am a messenger!" she called, her voice a high-pitched buzz. "I mean you no harm!" Amazed, Eli let the rocks fall to the ground. The insect landed and dipped her head in a quick bow. "Prince Eli," she began, "my name is Riley, and I fear that I bring you sad tidings. Your father is gravely ill."

"My father!" Eli exclaimed. "What happened?"

"The Great Syphon attacked the kingdom of Heverly," Riley answered.

"The golden serpent?" said Isabel. "But that's only a children's tale!"

"Alas, all too real," replied Riley mournfully. "The king was badly wounded in the battle and Syphon escaped. Your father's steward sent me to beg you to return home. He fears that your uncle Thornshackle may try to seize the throne while your father lies helpless."

Eli hesitated. "It was my father who turned his back on me when I told him I would marry Isabel and no one else," he said.

"But now he needs your help," Isabel said softly. "And so do the people of Heverly."

"Will you do it, Your Majesty?" Riley asked.

"Yes," Eli answered. "I could never abandon Heverly."

"Then climb on my back," Riley directed. "We must be off."

In the bushes nearby, a tall, gaunt figure was hidden. Two hobgoblins crouched at his feet. "Follow them," he ordered, pointing at Eli, Isabel, and Riley. "I don't want the prince to reach Heverly alive."

The hobgoblins bowed. "Yes, Lord Thornshackle," they hissed.

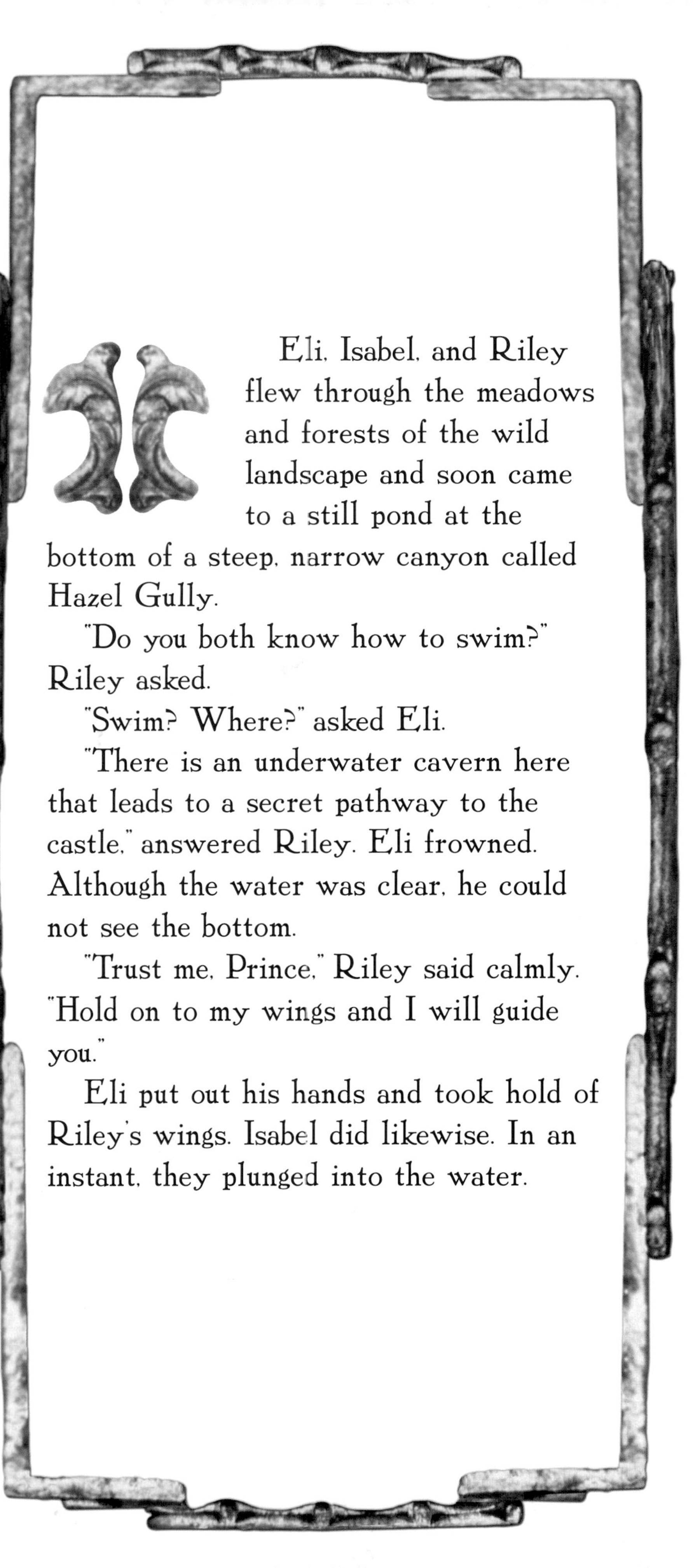

Eli, Isabel, and Riley flew through the meadows and forests of the wild landscape and soon came to a still pond at the bottom of a steep, narrow canyon called Hazel Gully.

"Do you both know how to swim?" Riley asked.

"Swim? Where?" asked Eli.

"There is an underwater cavern here that leads to a secret pathway to the castle," answered Riley. Eli frowned. Although the water was clear, he could not see the bottom.

"Trust me, Prince," Riley said calmly. "Hold on to my wings and I will guide you."

Eli put out his hands and took hold of Riley's wings. Isabel did likewise. In an instant, they plunged into the water.

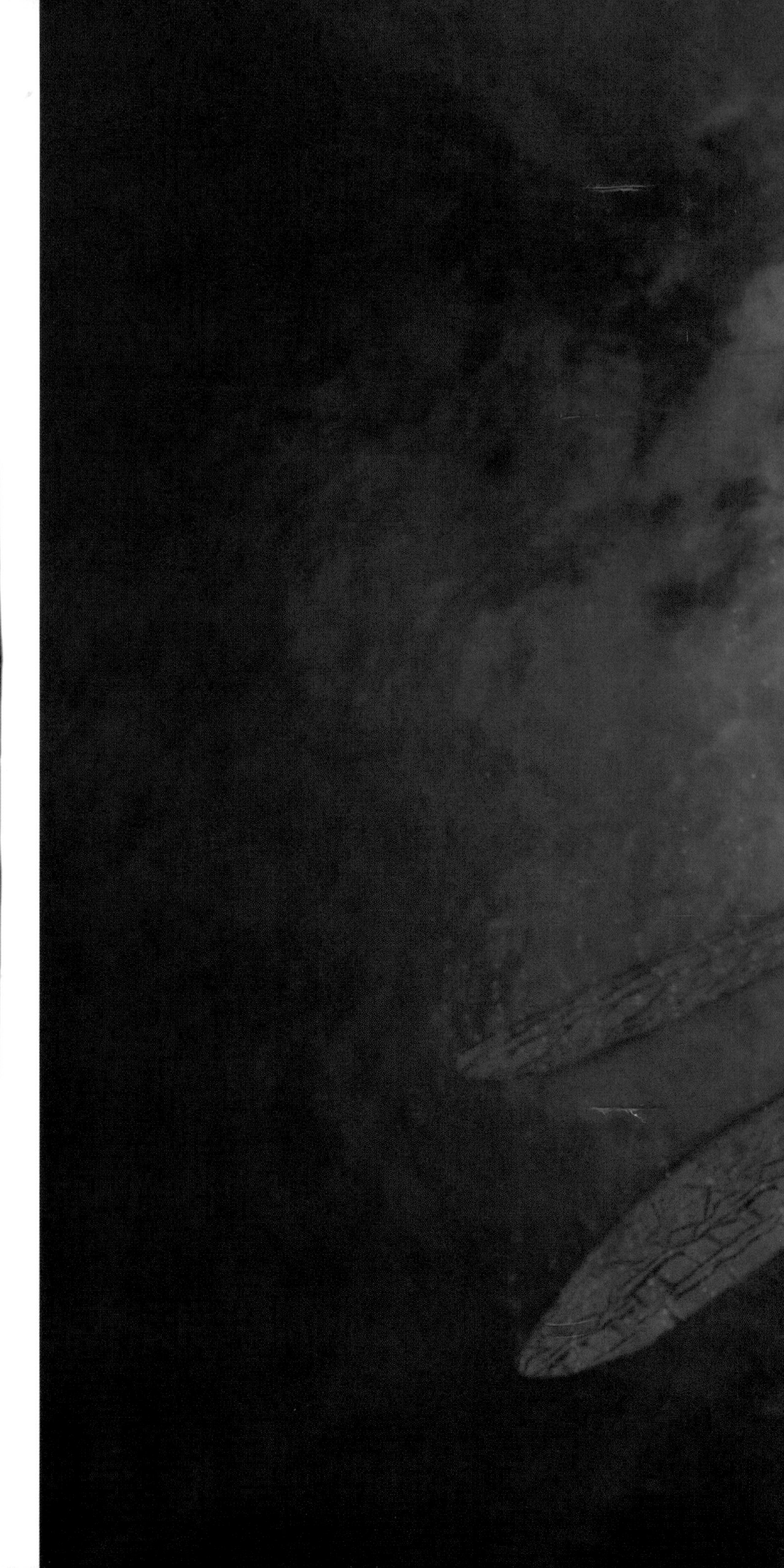

Gasping for air, the three burst to the surface and scrambled onto the rocky shore of a huge underwater cavern.

"We have entered the Crystal Cave," whispered Riley. Eli wrung out his sleeves as he looked up. Glistening stalactites made of razor-sharp glass hung from high above, while stalagmites grew up from the floor.

"Stay quiet," Riley warned. "Any sudden noise will send those ice daggers down upon us."

Close by, Thornshackle's goblins hid behind a large crystal. One of them lifted a stone.

"Not yet," hissed the other. "Wait until they've reached the middle of the cave." Then he whispered, "Now!"

The first goblin hurled the stone, striking the fragile glass above Eli and the others. In a thundering shower, the crystals shattered, crashing to the ground. A sharp crystal brushed Isabel's sleeve, slicing through the fabric.

"Grab on to my tail!" Riley shouted. Isabel and Eli held on as Riley wove through the falling glass and finally reached safety in a tunnel on the other side of the cave.

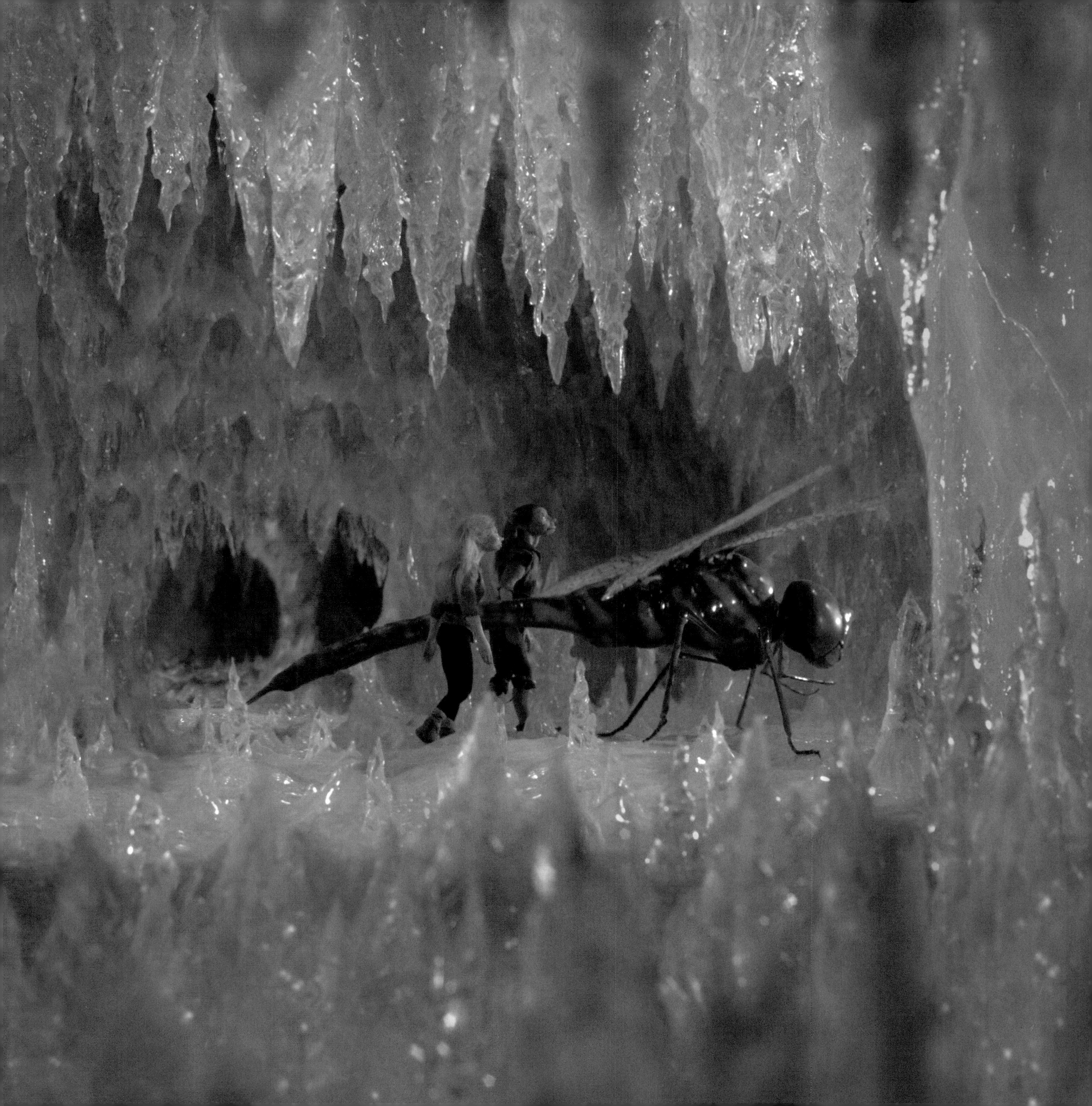

By nightfall, Eli had reached the castle and stood outside his father's chamber. He opened the door slowly and paused, listening to the voice of the king's steward, Dixon.

"Keep fighting, Your Majesty. Your strength grows with each passing day." Dixon turned when he heard footsteps behind him.

"Father?" Eli said as he rushed to the king's bedside.

"Prince Eli!" Dixon exclaimed, reaching out to embrace him. "I am so thankful you have returned."

"How is he, Dixon?" Eli spoke quietly.

"I am afraid he hasn't uttered a word in days."

Eli reached out and touched his father's arm. "Is he going to die?"

"Of that, I am unsure." Dixon frowned. "We have done all we can."

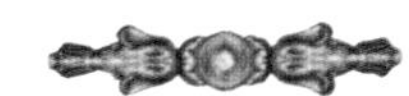

Later that night, Eli, Isabel, and Dixon walked together in the royal garden.

"You have always taught me that death is nothing to fear," Eli said to Dixon, "but how can you be sure?"

Dixon touched a small object hanging from a rosebush. "Do you see this cocoon?" he asked. "Inside lies a caterpillar that will soon transform. And just as it becomes something new, we too make a change when it is our time to pass on."

"It is too soon for my father to make that passage," Eli said desperately. "Is there nothing we can do? Perhaps a spell . . ."

Dixon shook his head. "Only the king himself and the power of his scepter could cast a spell strong enough to counter the poison of the serpent's bite."

"Not true." A deep voice startled them all. Isabel moved closer to Eli as Thornshackle stepped out of the shadows. "Greetings, Nephew," said Thornshackle. "Have you forgotten Scratch, the old crone? She may be a witch, but with her crystal orb she has power enough to cure the king—if someone could convince her to try."

"It's too dangerous," Dixon objected. "The journey to the Valley of the Skulls is perilous in itself. And Scratch is not to be trusted."

"Surely the prince is not afraid of such a harmless old soul?" Thornshackle mocked. "Or will you run away again, Nephew, as you did before?"

Eli met his uncle's gaze angrily. "I'll leave tomorrow," he answered back. Thornshackle gave him a wicked smile before slipping back into the shadows.

"I'm going with you!" Isabel declared.

"No," Eli said, staring after Thornshackle. In his mind's eye, Eli saw the fox, cheated of its prey, vanishing into smoke. "Isabel, you must stay. There is more than one danger at work here. You must help Dixon watch over my father until I can return."

Before Eli left the castle, he gathered royal jewels and gold into a satchel to offer Scratch in exchange for her help. For protection, Dixon gave him the king's sword. Then, on Riley's back, he traveled all day, soaring across the sky over jagged cliffs and winding rivers on his way to the Valley of the Skulls.

"We won't make the journey by the day's end!" shouted Eli to Riley over the buzz of her wings.

"We should find a place to rest for the night," Riley agreed. She headed down toward a wooded glen beneath them.

"What was it like growing up in the royal palace?" Riley asked Eli as they sat near a campfire he had made from the fallen branches of the surrounding cypress trees. "And tell me about your parents. Did they care deeply for one another?"

"Oh, yes. Very much," Eli answered. "My mother passed away when I was just a sprite. But I do remember how she admired my father, and he adored her as well. She was the only one who could make him laugh. She used to sing to me every night. I still remember the words." He recited:

Poppies and pansies, close your eyes;
Swifts and swallows and fireflies
Will bring you dreams till night is through.
When morning comes, I'll be with you.

"It's beautiful," Riley said.

"I only wish I could remember the melody," Eli said, shaking his head with regret.

"Maybe someday you will," Riley answered.

Riley and Eli started out early the next morning, and soon they reached a gray and desolate valley. Riley swooped down and headed for the gaping mouth of a cave at the base of a high cliff. Hearing a terrible shriek, Eli glanced up.

"Look out!" he shouted.

Out of the sky plunged a flock of flying spiders with batlike wings. The Rancids hovered, clawing and snapping at Eli and Riley.

"Don't stop!" cried Eli. "Fly inside!"

Riley soared into the open mouth of the cave and flew down a long passage as the Rancids followed closely behind. The tunnel ended suddenly and Riley landed, spinning around to face the horrible creatures. Eli leapt off her back, drawing his sword.

"That's enough!" called out a low, raspy voice. "You've brought me guests, now let me have a look at them!" It was Scratch, hobbling in for a closer look. "Ah, the royal prince," she said blushingly. "You've traveled all this way just to see me?"

Eli had never seen anyone as ugly as Scratch. Her hair was a mass of greasy tangles, and her teeth were filed down to sharp points. But Eli tried not to stare, and spoke courteously. "My father is ill. I've humbly come to ask for your help."

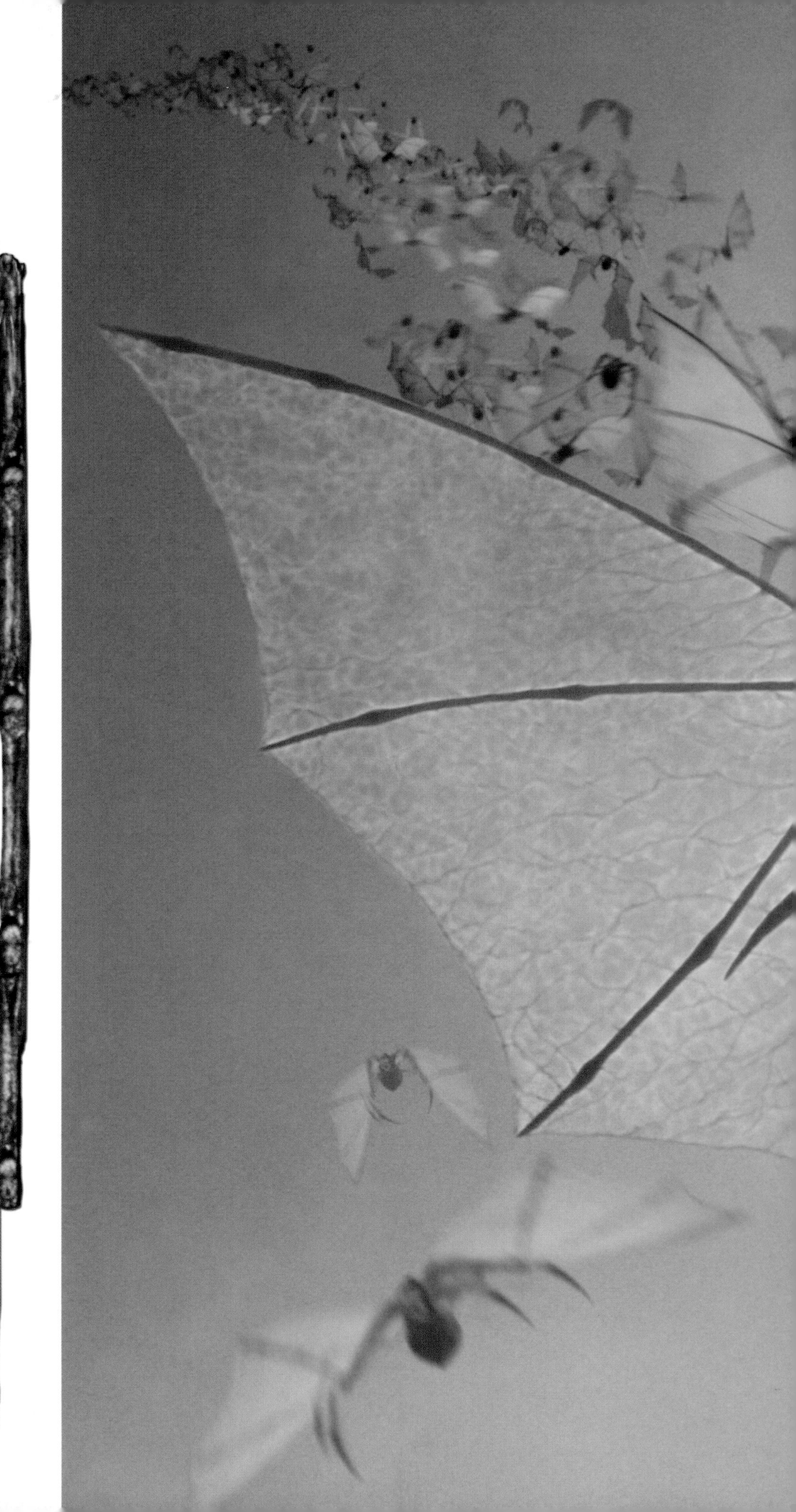

"Wait!" Scratch snapped. "News this important I must see for myself." She snatched her crystal orb from a table and held the magical globe to her forehead, then closed her eyes.

Eli watched in amazement as tiny images appeared and faded inside the orb. First, he saw a vision of the king's battle with Syphon, then his father lying sick in bed.

"And what can I expect in return for such a task as this?" Scratch said, lowering the orb.

Eli placed the jewel-filled satchel in front of her. "This is a small token of what I shall give you if you succeed."

Scratch rummaged through the treasures, cackling with glee. "I can help you, my dear. But it won't be easy. I must have the blood of the beast who caused your father's suffering."

Eli's eyes widened.

"I am too old to do battle with the great serpent myself," Scratch continued. "You must do it! Cut off the viper's golden rattle. Within it flows his blood. Bring it to me and I will concoct an antidote. Now, go!" she cried.

Eli jumped on Riley's back and they sped off down the tunnel. Once they were out of sight, Thornshackle emerged from hiding. "What if he makes it back unharmed?" he asked the old crone.

"He won't," she answered. "Even his own father's army couldn't defeat the golden serpent . . . but if by some miracle he does return, I have a plan."

Before long, Riley and Eli were flying over rocky terrain littered with hundreds of skeletons scattered about like fallen leaves.

"What is that odor?" Eli gasped, covering his nose.

"The smell of death," Riley replied. "The Valley of the Skulls gets its name from this place," she added. "Syphon is not an enemy to be taken lightly. Many have tried to defeat him and have failed."

"Like my father," Eli responded sadly.

"Look, there it is!" Riley shouted. "The Dark Rock!" Syphon's lair was a volcanic mountain as black as coal. Its jagged peaks towered high into the clouds.

An anxious tingle fluttered in Eli's stomach. "Are you coming with me?" he asked Riley.

"You know I cannot," she said regretfully. "The serpent's hot breath would turn my wings to ash. You must face Syphon alone."

Riley landed on a ledge where a narrow crack in the rocks led into the heart of the mountain. Taking a deep breath, Eli entered the passageway. He paused to light a torch. The walls around him were riddled with tiny holes, as if they were made of black sea coral. He thought he heard a deep, rhythmic sound, like breathing. Drawing his father's sword, he quietly crept forward.

Minutes passed and the flame of Eli's torch began to fade, as if the dark, musty air were choking it. Mysterious shadows seemed to follow him as they crawled across the rock, then vanished into the cracks. Eli's torch flickered out just as the narrow passage opened up into a vast cavern. But burning embers scattered throughout the cave gave off enough light so that he could still see.

Eli crouched down to touch a large, segmented shape that lay at his feet. It was as light as an empty seed pod—a serpent's rattle. Others were strewn about, but they were as dry as the one in his hands. None held the blood for Scratch's potion.

A flash of gold between two rock pillars caught Eli's eye, and he heard a low vibrating hum. He realized that it was the warning rattle of Syphon, but before he could move, the serpent exploded from a crack in the wall. Syphon's shimmering golden coils wrapped around Eli, squeezing him tightly. As the creature lifted Eli high into the air, his father's sword slipped from his grasp. Eli was now face-to-face with the most feared enemy of the kingdom.

Syphon had not one, but three heads, which swayed hypnotically before Eli's horrified gaze. The head on the left opened his mouth, revealing lethal fangs, and spoke in a slow, sinister hiss. "Who are you? And why have you foolishly trespassed here?"

"I am Prince Eli. I've come from the kingdom to make you an offer," he replied.

"An offer, you say? And what might that be?" The second head spoke as eerily as the first, and his breath was unbearably wretched.

"It's your rattle I want," Eli blurted out. "Of course, not if it is still a part of you. But I notice you shed them from time to time. I'd pay you handsomely for the next one that falls away."

Syphon's three heads roared with the most wicked laughter, sending echoes throughout the labyrinth. The third head smiled with a venomous grin and leaned close to Eli, whispering, "Look around you, Prince. What need have we of gold?"

"I'm hungry," growled the first head. "Let's eat him and be done with it!"

Thinking quickly, Eli had an idea. "Wait!" he cried desperately. "If I am going to die, then it must be in a way that befits my royal blood. The wisest and mightiest of you must take the first bite."

Syphon's heads glanced at one another. "Well spoken, Prince," hissed the third head. "So it shall be—I will take the first bite."

"What do you mean, you?" snapped the second head, spinning around to face him. "If any of us is better, it's me!" he grumbled with anger.

"Out of my way! I am the greatest of us three!" proclaimed the first.

Eli's plan was working. Syphon's three heads started to bicker and snarl at one another and the coils around Eli began to loosen. He shifted his body back and forth, and with one final move, he fell from the serpent's grasp. He seized his father's sword and swung it at Syphon's tail, instantly severing the golden rattle from its body. All three heads howled in pain and then one cried out, "After him!"

Eli grabbed the oozing rattle and ran, diving headfirst into a tunnel that was too small for Syphon to follow. His jaws snapped shut just inches from Eli's heels, and the serpent's roar of fury shook the mountain around him. Eli scrambled to his feet and ran fiercely down the black tunnel, which came to an abrupt end.

His eyes darted around in the darkness, searching for a way out. As he looked up, he saw a faint gleam of light high above. Digging his fingers into the crumbling rock, he climbed toward it. The light grew brighter, and soon Eli could see that it was coming from a hole in the side of the mountain.

Eli was within arm's reach of the hole when he heard a great crash below. Rocks flew as Syphon burst into the tunnel and began to hoist his massive body upward. With no time to lose, Eli lunged for the hole and forced his head and shoulders out into the sunlight. But the hole was too small and he couldn't pull himself the rest of the way through. "Riley!" he shouted. "Help me!"

Eli could feel Syphon's hot breath on his legs as he heard the serpent's mocking laughter. "What have we here, a pair of dancing twigs?" the first head cackled.

"The tastiest twigs we've ever encounted, I'll wager," said the second.

"And no doubt there's a juicy reward at the end of them," said the third. Then all three laughed and opened their mouths wide, preparing to bite.

But as Eli despaired, Riley suddenly soared over a rocky ledge. Eli desperately clutched onto her tail. Riley's wings beat with the force of a hurricane as she yanked Eli free just in time. And Syphon, thrusting forward to attack Eli, hit the top of the shaft with such force that it sent the ceiling crashing down on him.

Riley and Eli flew as fast and as far as they could until the Dark Rock looked like a pebble on the horizon. Within a short time, they were back at Scratch's cave.

"Here is what you asked for, Scratch. Now make your potion!" said Eli, thrusting Syphon's golden rattle at her.

Scratch had gasped in surprise to see him enter her cave, but now that she had the rattle in her hands, she smiled. "You may be brave, young prince, but you're not too smart," she said, then took the rattle and cracked it open, pouring the golden liquid into a chalice. She brought the cup to her lips and drank it down in one gulp. Instantly her skin grew smooth, her hair soft and long, and her face young and lovely.

"Am I not more pleasing to you than before?" Scratch asked in the same raspy voice Eli had heard from the crone.

"You've tricked me!" he cried.

"Indeed I have," she replied, "and now I am more powerful than ever."

Eli drew his sword and backed away, but the Rancids were already waiting at the cave's entrance and he was trapped.

"Not so fast, my handsome prince. I have plans for you," Scratch said with a wicked smile.

Thornshackle suddenly appeared from the darkness. He held Isabel tightly with one hand, while the other was clasped over her mouth.

"Drop your sword, Eli, or I will feed your precious Isabel to these hungry mouths," said Thornshackle, thrusting Isabel toward the horrible Rancids.

Eli hesitated. He could see no way to reach Isabel in time. Slowly he lowered his sword.

"Excellent," Scratch said. "Now *I* will become your queen, and together we will have a son who will rule the kingdom of Heverly."

"What?" Thornshackle shouted. He shoved Isabel away as he turned to face Scratch. "The throne belongs to me!"

At that moment, Riley burst into the cave, scattering the Rancids. Her powerful tail knocked over everything in her path. In the chaos, Isabel snatched the crystal orb from the table. Eli grabbed her hand and the two leapt onto Riley's back as she dodged the angry Rancids and escaped down the tunnel.

"Follow them!" Scratch commanded. Several of the Rancids lifted Scratch and Thornshackle into the air, carrying them out of the cave and after Riley.

Once outside, the Rancids dove at Riley, forcing her to land on top of the high cliff that loomed over Scratch's cave. Eli and Isabel toppled off her back as the Rancids dropped Thornshackle and Scratch beside them.

Scratch thrust her arms into the air and, instantly, dark clouds formed in the sky. Then a bolt of lightning struck her, but she was not consumed. Eli and the others watched in horror as her body grew taller. Her arms stretched outward, long and thin, while deadly claws sprouted from her fingertips. In an instant, Scratch was transformed into a hideous insectlike creature.

Eli stepped in front of Isabel and raised his sword, but the creature only laughed. "Do you think a mere metal sword can stop me?"

Then Isabel whispered to Eli. "The orb!" She raised it up. "Destroy it!"

Scratch shrieked in terror as Eli took the crystal orb and held it for a moment over the abyss.

"Eli! Don't be a fool!" Thornshackle shouted urgently. "The orb holds more power than you can imagine! Give it to me and we shall rule together."

Eli looked at his uncle, but then flung the sphere with all his might over the edge. Thornshackle lunged to save the magic crystal, but slipped and fell, screaming, toward the rocks below.

As the orb smashed against the rocks, Scratch cried out and then withered back into an ugly hag. The Rancids hovering above were changed into harmless doves and flew away, free at last.

Eli advanced on Scratch, threatening her with his sword. "Tell me how to save my father's life!" he demanded as the old crone cowered at the cliff's edge.

"Fool!" she cried, cringing from his blade. "Even I didn't have the power to heal. Only the king and his scepter can perform that kind of miracle."

"But my father is near death," said Eli.

Scratch replied, "And now, the power is passed on . . ."

"To me," Eli said softly. "The power is passed on to me."

At that moment, Eli realized, as rightful heir to the throne, he might be able to save his father himself.

"Hurry, Your Majesty!" shouted Riley.

Isabel and Eli climbed on Riley's back and the three soared off toward Heverly.

"Bring me my father's scepter at once." Eli pleaded with Dixon to hurry as he stood over his father. The king's face had lost all signs of life and Eli feared he had reached Heverly too late.

Dixon hastily brought the scepter into the king's chamber and gave it to Eli. The prince waved the scepter over his father's body. A moment passed, but nothing happened. Once again he tried, but still nothing.

"Be confident," urged Isabel. "Command the scepter."

Eli closed his eyes and said, "I have the power to be king." Suddenly the tip of the scepter glowed a brilliant red and his father's eyes began to open. The king looked at his son and smiled weakly.

"You came back," said the weary king.

"Yes, Father," Eli replied tenderly. He reached out to return the scepter, but the king shook his head.

"No. You have proved your right to wield it," he said. "But most of all, you've proved your love. And now it is my turn to prove mine." The king turned to Isabel. "Come here, my dear." He took Isabel's and Eli's hands and joined them together. "I am sorry for not recognizing what was before me. You have my blessing to wed." Eli looked up at Isabel and smiled.

"I only wish I could stay long enough for your wedding day," the king said, laying his head back down on the pillow. "But it is my time to go." Then the king slowly vanished away, leaving only the crumpled linen on the bed where he had lain.

Eli bowed his head in sorrow. "Now both of my parents have gone away," he said quietly, "and I am forever without them."

"Not entirely," said Dixon.

"What do you mean?" Eli responded.

"Do you remember the night in the garden and what I told you about the cocoon?" asked Dixon.

"It will change," Eli answered, and turned his eyes back toward his father's empty bed. A soft humming began to drift into the room from the open door to the balcony. Then a voice began to sing a tune Eli thought he had forgotten:

Poppies and pansies, close your eyes;
Swifts and swallows and fireflies
Will bring you dreams till night is through.
When morning comes, I'll be with you.

Eli rushed outside to see Riley hovering overhead. "Mother?" he whispered.

"Yes," answered Riley. "It is I."

Eli smiled at her and tears filled his eyes. "You were with me all along."

"I will always watch over you, my son," said Riley. "And so will your father."

Another dragonfly drifted down to hover beside Riley, and spoke in a familiar voice. "It is time, my dear."

"Where are you going?" asked Eli.

"Our life here has passed and tonight we must travel beyond the sea to our new home," Riley answered. "Take good care of yourself and your newfound kingdom."

Then the other dragonfly spoke. Farewell, my son . . . the king."

Eli smiled and waved good-bye as the two magnificent creatures turned away and flew off toward the setting sun.

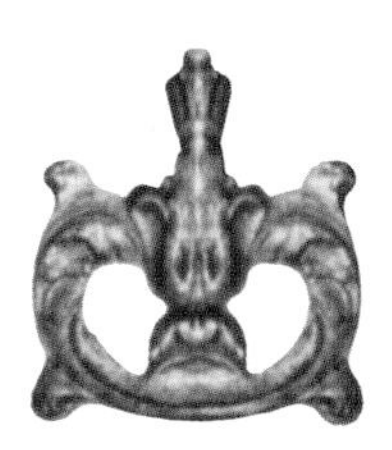

To my daughter, Catie, and my wife, Catherine, with love
—K. Y.

ACKNOWLEDGMENTS
The author would like to thank the following people
who, with their hard work and dedication
helped to bring this book to life:
Mark Yagher, Jeff Yagher, Bryan Sides, Mitch Coughlin,
Mario Torres, Tony Acosta, Dave Miner, Pete Konig, Gary Tunnicliffe,
David Reuther, Andrea Spooner, and Elaine Scott.

SEASTAR BOOKS
A division of NORTH-SOUTH BOOKS INC.

First published in the United States by SeaStar Books,
a division of North-South Books Inc., New York.
Published simultaneously in Canada, Australia, and New Zealand
by North-South Books, an imprint of Nord-Süd Verlag AG, Gossau Zürich, Switzerland.

Library of Congress Cataloging-in-Publication Data is available.

The artwork for this book was prepared by creating miniature sets and models
that were photographed, and then effects were added on computer using Adobe Photoshop software.

ISBN 1-58717-062-0 (trade binding)
1 3 5 7 9 TB 10 8 6 4 2
ISBN 1-58717-063-9 (library binding)
1 3 5 7 9 LB 10 8 6 4 2

Printed at South China Printing Co. LTD. in Hong Kong.

For more information about our books, and the authors and artists who create them,
visit our web site: www.northsouth.com